This is my dad

For Louise Brooks and Teacher
Librarians like her everywhere who
tirelessly share their book-love
with children.
– D.P.

For my friends Sami, Sue and Relle,
who are all the most remarkable
role models for their kids.
– N.J.

First published 2022

EK Books
an imprint of Exisle Publishing Pty Ltd
PO Box 864, Chatswood, NSW 2057, Australia
226 High Street, Dunedin, 9016, New Zealand
www.ekbooks.org

A CiP record for this book is available from the National
Library of Australia.

ISBN 978-1-922539-07-6

Designed by Mark Thacker
Typeset in Minya Nouvelle 16 on 26pt
Printed in China

This book uses paper sourced under ISO 14001 guidelines
from well-managed forests and other controlled sources.

10 9 8 7 6 5 4 3 2 1

This is my dad

The perfect dad isn't always a father

DIMITY POWELL & NICKY JOHNSTON

Leo loved Show and Tell, but when
his teacher, Miss Reilly, announced the topic,
Leo's tummy belly-flopped.

'Can our dads be part of our presentations?' Harper asked.

'Great idea,' Miss Reilly beamed. 'Let's invite them
along to celebrate with us!'

The classroom busied and buzzed.
Dads sounded important and special and ... fun!

Except to Leo, who burrowed into the quiet corner.
How can I celebrate someone I've never met? he worried.

Perhaps Mama would know.

'Mama?'

'Hang on. Rescue in progress!'

'Mama?'

'Not long now. Just one more chapter …'

'MaMA!'

'Almost there!'

That night, while Mama hunted
dragons and arrested aliens,
Leo waded through oceans of photos.

He dredged up every birthday card he had ever received.
He rummaged through his keep-forever treasures
but he could not find what he was looking for ...

Who is my dad? wondered Leo, imagining a world-renowned-surgeon dad or a first-class-hydrochute-inspector dad.

Or even just a Frisbee-throwing dad.

Leo did not have a cool, courageous, clever dad.
Leo did not have any kind of dad at all.

So, he asked Mr Ariti next door to help him celebrate. Mr Ariti shook his head, 'I'm too old to be your dad,' he said. 'What about him?'

But Sir Barkalot had already been to school.

The night before '*TELL US ABOUT YOUR DAD DAY*',
Leo slumped over his empty notebook.
Who was he going to talk about?

'There!' declared Mama.
'Planet Earth saved, again!'

Suddenly, Leo had an idea ...

Leo's tummy churned as he wobbled to the front of the classroom, gulped down a giant breath and said in his bravest voice ...

'My dad is amazing.'

'My dad's scared of spiders but eats monsters for breakfast.'

'My dad discovers new galaxies every Friday night after making my favourite pizza.'

'My dad knows the way to places that are out of this world ... *and* ... how to get home again.'

'My dad can't throw Frisbees but has the softest kisses in the universe.'

'My dad is my everything.'

'This is my dad ...'